The Owls of Blossom Wood

First published in the UK in 2015 by Scholastic Children's Books

An imprint of Scholastic Ltd
Euston House, 24 Eversholt Street
London, NW1 1DB, UK
Registered office: Westfield Road, Southam, Warwickshire, CV47 0RA

ISBN 978 1407 15663 7

A CIP catalogue record for this book is available from the British Library

Printed and bound by CPI Group (UK) Ltd, Croydon, CR0 4YY
Papers used by Scholastic Children's Books are made from wood grown in sustainable forests.

7 9 10 8 6

www.scholastic.co.uk

The Owls of Blossom Wood

A Magical Beginning

Catherine Coe

SCHOLASTIC

Blossom Wood
Brown Desert
Willow Lake
Apple Orchard
Pine Forest
Foxglove Glade

Echo Mountains
Badger Falls
Rushing River
Moon Chestnut
Oval of Oaks
The Great Hedge

For Katelyn Hope Henry.
Always remembered xxx

Chapter 1

An Amazing Discovery

Katie's long blonde hair billowed out as she spun round her bedroom. She was showing her two best friends the new ballet dance she'd learnt that week.

Eva and Alex sat on Katie's bed, clapping as Katie finished and did a curtsy. Eva's emerald-green eyes returned to her sketchpad, where she was halfway

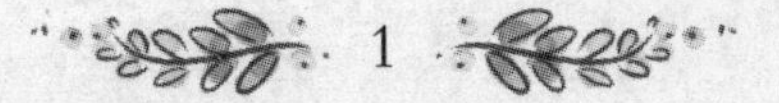

through a drawing of a rabbit eating a banana.

Alex peered over at Eva's drawing. The rabbit was so lifelike, it looked as if it might jump off the page. "You're brilliant at drawing," she said. "I wish I was that good. But … you know rabbits don't eat bananas."

"Really? Oops." Eva turned to Katie,

who was now upside down, doing handstands against her bedroom door. "Can I borrow a rubber?"

Katie flung her long legs back to the floor. "If I can find—" She stopped mid-sentence and put her ear to the door. "It's Alfie," she mouthed silently.

The girls froze and listened. *BANG,*

BANG, BANG went the door.

"I wish he'd just play by himself," whispered Katie. Her younger brother was always pestering them.

Alex bit her lip. "Maybe we should let him in?"

Katie groaned. "I do loads of stuff with him when you're not here. Remember what happened last time? He broke the bead necklaces Eva made for us!"

"So what should we do?" Eva adjusted the loom-band butterfly clip in her bobbed brown hair. "We can't go to mine – no one's there."

Alex lowered her eyes. "Nor mine. Sorry."

The girls lived next door to each other in a quiet countryside village. To the right of Katie's ivy-covered house stood a red-brick bungalow where Alex lived. On the left was Eva's ramshackle thatched cottage. The two girls often came over to Katie's after school, while their parents were still at work. They'd been friends for as long as they could remember.

"Well, I don't want to be stuck hiding in *here* all day." Katie put her hands on her hips.

Alex pressed her head to the door. "Wait – I think Alfie's gone."

Eva frowned in concentration. "I think I can hear the TV in the living room."

"You're right!" Katie said, her mouth stretching into a beam. "Let's sneak outside..." She twisted the doorknob silently, and tiptoed out to the landing. She could hear the loud laughter of a cartoon.

The three girls tottered over to the stairs. Katie pointed at a step in the middle. "Watch that one," she mouthed. "It creaks."

They stepped down carefully, but somehow in the middle Eva stumbled on a stair and slid to the bottom. She clamped her mouth shut, careful not to make a sound, while Alex and Katie stifled giggles at their clumsy friend. The three girls darted through the hallway, past Katie's dad at his laptop in the kitchen, and out

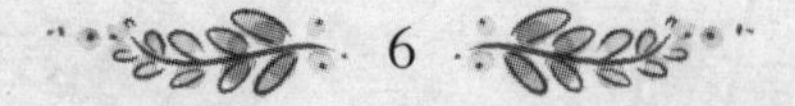

into the garden. Yellow afternoon sunshine flooded the lawn, and the grass felt warm and springy under their bare feet.

"Can we sit in the hammocks?" Eva darted towards the cherry trees where Katie's mum had tied up hammocks. But a tug on her T-shirt jolted her back and she swung round. Katie was shaking her head and pointing at the living-room window. The hammocks were right in front of it! "Sorry," Eva whispered.

"What's that over there?" Alex's big brown eyes had turned to something lying far away at the end of the garden.

"It's an old chestnut tree that fell down ages ago," Katie explained. "Mum keeps saying she should get rid of it, but she never has."

Eva was already skipping towards the abandoned tree. "This is the perfect

place – Alfie can't see us at all from here."

Katie sprinted to catch Eva up, with Alex not far behind. Katie's garden was enormous, and they passed the washing line, rabbit hutch, rose bed and greenhouse before reaching the tree trunk. It lay amongst tangles of long grass and wild flowers – pretty poppies, bluebells, daisies and violets.

Eva plonked herself on one end of the trunk and ran her hands across the peeling bark. "I wonder how old the tree was."

"You can tell the age of a tree by the number of rings inside the trunk," said Alex, who loved wildlife and nature. She wandered through the long grasses to the end of the trunk – and gasped, "Huh?"

"What's up?" Katie ran to join Alex.

"Wow – it's hollow!" Katie began crawling into the trunk. "It's huge in here." Her voice echoed, as if she were in a cave.

As Katie's feet disappeared inside, Eva poked her head in. She started climbing in, then glanced back over her shoulder at Alex. "Come on – it'll be fun!"

Alex wasn't so sure – but at that moment she heard a loud shout from the top of the garden. Alfie! She dived into the trunk before he could see her.

Inside, the gnarled old tree trunk seemed even bigger than it looked from the outside, and the girls could move along it easily. Katie sat at one end, cross-legged and grinning from ear to ear, while Eva crouched in the middle. Alex scrambled in close to them.

"We'll be safe in here." Katie's blue eyes

twinkled like diamonds in the dark.

Eva grabbed both her friends' hands. "This is brilliant. Our very own secret den!"

Alex looked around as her eyes adjusted to the shadows. She spotted a large, pure-white feather nestling on the side of the trunk. With her free hand she plucked it up. "Where did this come from?"

"It looks like a—" But before Katie could finish, the tree shuddered. The girls squeezed each other's hands.

"Um, what's happening?" asked Eva. "Is that Alfie?"

They quickly realized it wasn't when the trunk seemed to start turning, as if they were on a roundabout. Air blasted around their heads as though a train were rushing past. What was going on?

Alex let out a squeal, Eva screamed and Katie laughed nervously. "Is this some kind of joke?" she gulped, though she couldn't think how anyone could do this.

The trunk spun and spun and spun some more, and the wind buffeted them around. The friends clamped their eyes shut, hoping that it would soon stop. Round and round they went. Eva felt as if she were inside one of her baby sister's rattles.

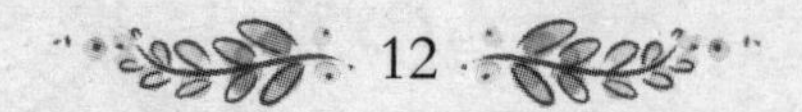

Alex felt her toes tingling, like really bad pins and needles. But at least the spinning seemed to be getting slower. Then her ears started to itch, and her hands felt … well … *weird*. Softer.

"Is it over?" Katie's usually loud voice was a whisper.

The spinning had stopped completely now, but Alex didn't dare open her eyes.

Chapter 2
Welcome to Blossom Wood

It was only Eva's yelps that made Alex look. She shut her eyes again immediately. *I must be dreaming*, she told herself.

"Alex, look. Look!" It was Katie's voice this time. Except it wasn't really Katie. It was… Alex opened her eyes just a slit. No, it couldn't be.

"This is amazing!" squealed Eva.

Alex took a long, deep breath, then opened her eyes properly. She froze in disbelief. Next to her stood a beautiful white owl with a heart-shaped face and light-brown wings. "Eva, is that really you?" she asked.

The beautiful bird nodded and opened

her beak. "It's me!" she tweeted. "But I'm … I'm a … barn owl!"

Behind Eva, another large owl, this one covered in pure white feathers with black flecks, bounced from foot to foot. Alex gasped. "*Katie?*"

"Yep!" Katie jumped closer and put a wing on Alex's. "I think I'm a snowy owl, right?"

Alex bobbed her head. "You definitely look like one! But is this really happening? Where are we?" She craned her neck to look up at her friends – and then down at herself. She was tiny compared to them, with fluffy brown and white feathers and thin stick legs. *I'm a little owl!* she thought.

Katie swivelled her head around, and her orange owl eyes grew very wide. "Um, maybe don't look down, but I

think we're up in a tree!"

The three friends grabbed each other's wings as they realized they were teetering on a tree branch. A branch high in a forest that stretched as far as their eyes could see.

They stared and stared and stared. Down on the forest floor they could see little grey rabbits scampering about and deer weaving between the trees. Pretty little bees buzzed around flowers and hives, while cute brown birds fluttered their wings so fast they were blurs. Trees of every size and shape stretched upwards towards the bright-blue, cloudless sky, some with large glossy leaves, some with long thin draping leaves, some weighed down with fruits, some covered in brightly coloured blooms. A rich, leafy smell filled the air, mixed with the scent of fruit and flowers. Sunshine poured down between the trees, creating spots of light which made everything look extra magical.

Eva's small pale pink beak had fallen open in wonder. "What *is* this place – and how did we get here?"

"Ahem," came a cough from below them. "I think I can probably help you there."

The owls looked down. At the base of the tree stood a badger, his stripy head

bowed, looking a little sheepish.

"I'm terribly sorry if I shocked you," he continued in a deep, gravelly voice. "But I am so, so glad and grateful that you're here. Would you mind awfully coming down to talk? It's just with these old, tired legs I can't climb trees the way I used to."

Although they were more than a little bit surprised at the arrival of a talking badger, he seemed friendly enough, and was certainly very polite. What's more, Alex, Katie and Eva were desperate to find out what was going on. They began hopping from branch to branch, towards the ground. It felt a bit scary at first, balancing on the tree, but they soon realized their talons could grip the branches tightly, and they didn't need to worry about falling off.

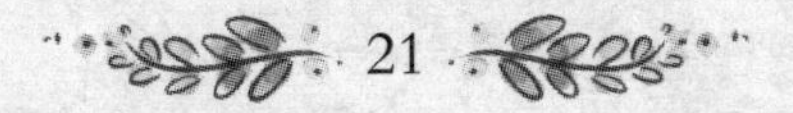

As they leapt to the floor, making the leaves on the ground rustle, the badger smiled. From behind him, with a flourish, he produced three acorn cups. "I expect you're parched from the journey – please, have some elderberry tea to quench your thirst."

"Thank you." Katie grinned and reached out a wing to take one of the little nut cups. She liked this badger.

"You knew we were coming?" Eva asked, tipping her feathery head to the side. "How?"

The badger's shoulders slumped. "Well, you see, we've been awaiting your arrival for a very long time. The feather – I presume you saw it?"

The three friends nodded as they slurped their tea through their beaks. It was delicious – like warm fruit squash – and smelt lovely, too.

"I kept sending out the feather,

hoping the sign would one day be answered. You see, here in Blossom Wood, we've been without owls for many years. Indeed, I'm older than I'd like to admit, and I can't remember owls ever being around."

Eva's heart-shaped face creased in a frown. "But why do you need owls?"

The badger twitched his shiny black nose. "You're very modest. Everyone knows owls are the wisest creatures of the wood, able to help with the most impossible of problems. Thank treetops that you're here at last."

"But we *will* be able to go back home again, won't we?" Alex said, unable to stop her soft voice wobbling as she spoke.

"Well, I hope you won't leave just yet. Blossom Wood needs you! But I'm sure you'll be able to leave just the way you

came – by the very same branch of the chestnut tree." The kind badger smiled. "Where exactly did you come from, anyway?"

The friends looked at each other, not knowing what to say.

"Umm..." Katie decided it would be best to tell the truth. "From my garden … we somehow got here – and we were owls!"

"I can see that!" The badger chuckled. "I might be old but there's nothing wrong with my eyesight. Frommy Garden? I haven't heard of the place, I'm afraid. Never mind – the most important thing is that you're here now to help us."

Oh dear, thought Alex. The badger hadn't understood what Katie had meant at all!

"What is it you need help with, Mr

Badger?" Eva asked, before tipping the last of her tea into her beak. She missed slightly and spilt a few drops down her white feathery body, wiping them away with a wing.

"Oh, do call me Bobby. I'm sorry, how rude of me – I should have introduced myself at the beginning! May I ask your names?"

"I'm Katie," Katie said, shaking Bobby's paw with her snowy-white wingtip.

Eva put out a brown wing. "I'm Eva."

Alex hopped forward shyly on one of her stick-like legs. "And I'm Alex."

"It's an honour to meet you, Katie, Eva and Alex." Bobby leant back on his rear legs and folded into a bow. "Now, did you notice our chestnut tree?" The badger pointed a paw to the tree they'd arrived on and his black eyes grew serious.

"It's the tallest, oldest tree in the forest, and the most-loved, too. We believe it must be magical to have lived so long. And see how its trunk curves like a crescent moon? We call it the Moon Chestnut. Every baby creature who's born in the wood is brought to the hollow at the bottom of the tree to be blessed with a long life. It's been home to all sorts of creatures for thousands of years. Indeed, many birds and animals still live in its branches today. The problem is … it's dying!"

Katie, Alex and Eva stared upwards. Bobby was right – this enormous, curved tree, unlike all the others, had brown, drooping leaves, and its branches were thin and brittle. They could see lots of bird nests and squirrel nests and even a beehive right near the top. What would happen to those if the tree died?

The badger breathed a deep, grumbling sigh. "It's a very grave problem, because many creatures live in the tree. They don't want to lose their home – and we don't want our beloved, magical tree to die. It's a completely desperate situation!"

Despite the warm sun on her back, Alex felt icy cold with worry. She wanted to help, but she had no idea what to do – she knew quite a lot about different trees, but not how to save them!

Eva spotted a little shiny chestnut on

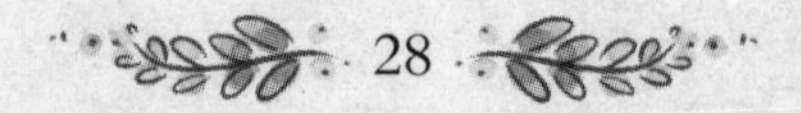

the ground and picked it up in her talon. The smooth nut felt much smaller than ordinary chestnuts, and she couldn't see any more around – not on the tree, nor beneath it.

A rustling sound made them all jump. A grey squirrel with a big, bushy tail wearing a cute little blouse came bounding through a blackberry bush. "You've found one!" she squeaked, her tail twitching from side to side. "Can I have it, pretty please?"

Eva dropped the tiny chestnut into the squirrel's paws and she gobbled it up in one bite. Eva noticed Bobby frowning at the creature.

"Loulou, please don't be so very rude! I know the Moon Chestnut hardly grows any nuts these days, but the owls are here to help us and all you can do is think about your stomach!"

The squirrel's furry grey cheeks flamed red. "Oh, I'm so, so, so, so, so, so, so sorry!" She lowered her tail and did a strange sort of squirrel curtsy. Eva couldn't help but giggle.

Bobby tutted at the squirrel, then turned to Katie, Eva and Alex. "Let me offer my sincere apologies too."

"Please don't worry about it," said Eva.

"The wood has a much more serious problem right now."

Alex nodded her little fluffy head in agreement. "Perhaps we could have a meeting with all the animals in the wood about saving the Moon Chestnut?"

Bobby clapped his leathery black paws together. "That sounds like a marvellous plan. Loulou, can you start getting the message out to everyone? We'll have it in the usual place – Foxglove Glade."

"Consider it done, Bobby!" Loulou grinned and scampered away up the curved Moon Chestnut trunk, calling out to all the creatures she passed. "Meeting at Foxglove Glade! Please spread the word!"

Birds poked their heads from their nests, bees buzzed out of their hives, and butterflies emerged from behind branches. They all began racing away into the forest.

"I'll meet you there," Bobby said to the owls. "You'll be much speedier than an old badger like me, so it's best if I get a head start. Fly over Pine Forest, past Apple Orchard, then go left by Willow Lake and you won't miss it." He lumbered off along a narrow path, heading for the towering pine trees in the distance.

Katie, Eva and Alex turned to each other. They were all thinking the same thing, though Katie was the first to say it. "He said *fly*. We're going to fly!"

Chapter 3
Let's Fly

Katie unravelled her huge white wings and flapped furiously. Nothing happened. "Come on," she said to herself. "Flying can't be that hard!" She batted at the air again, jumping at the same time, but she quickly landed with a thump on the leafy ground. A giant bubble of disappointment rose up inside her. "Why can't I fly?!"

Alex stood on one leg, frowning. "If you can't do it, with your massive wings, I've got no chance with mine." She opened up her little brown wings and fluttered them about. To her surprise, she floated a few centimetres off the ground. Alex giggled shyly in excitement, although she felt bad for Katie.

"I guess you're only small, so your wings don't need to be very big either,"

twittered Eva. She stretched out her silky wings and flapped them gently. She skipped along, and felt her feet begin to lift upwards. "Tu-whit tu-whoo!" she cried as she batted her wings to fly higher. "This is amazing!"

Katie's orange eyes drooped sadly. "What's wrong with my wings?"

Eva fluttered back down to the ground. "You might just need a bit of practice – and patience." Eva gave Alex a little wink. Katie didn't like to do anything slowly.

She widened her beautiful wings once more, and this time she moved them through the air more carefully.

"Try running a little," Alex suggested. "But not too fast."

Determined, Katie stared ahead and began jogging along. Her giant white

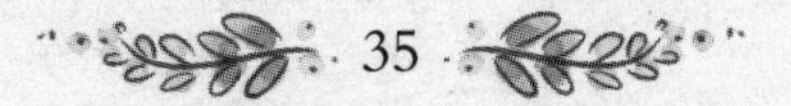

wings ruffled the air as she guided them up and down. Then she let out a squeal – she was suddenly soaring upwards, her feathers rippling as she flew. "I did it!"

"Come on." Eva smiled and nudged Alex with her wing. "Let's catch her up."

"Yes – we need to get to Foxglove Glade. Otherwise Bobby *will* be there before us!"

Side by side, they skipped and flapped their wings. Eva felt herself rise up on the gentle breeze, Alex just behind her. Eva fluttered her wings faster, the wind whistling past her feathery ears. She tilted and twisted to avoid tree trunks and branches, and the woods grew smaller and smaller beneath her. Blossom Wood seemed to stretch for ever, and looked even more magical from above. She could see a sparkling river winding through a

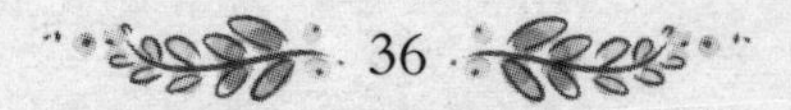

yellow-flowered valley in the distance, and to her right a mountain range rose up, its peaks dusted with white.

The three friends' faces ached from grinning as they zoomed through the sky.

Katie dipped her head, tipped up her long white tail, and did a loop-the-loop. "Look at meeeee!" she cried.

"Let me try!" Eva tilted forward into a spin – but found herself hurtling into a pine tree. She flapped her wings in a panic and shot upwards, just avoiding it. "That was close!"

Alex didn't dare fly upside down like her friends, but she did manage to flutter her wings so quickly she could then glide along, like a little fluffy kite. It felt incredible to be able to float on the air. She looked down, remembering Bobby's

directions. "Look – we've come to the end of the pine trees. We've got to go past Apple Orchard next, then turn left by Willow Lake."

They sped over the huge green orchard. The trees were ripe with every kind of apple imaginable – pink shiny ones, giant green ones, red waxy ones.

"There's the lake." Katie pointed a snowy-white wing at the blue water of Willow Lake. Glistening in the sunshine, it was dotted with shiny, pale-green lily pads. Willow trees crowded at the edge of its shore, their silvery leaves dangling like beautiful curtains around it.

Alex bobbed her little head to the left as they passed the lake. "That looks like the glade."

Foxglove Glade was so beautiful it took Eva's breath away. A large circle of short green grass was surrounded by the prettiest flowers in a rainbow of colours. The foxgloves swayed gently in the warm breeze, as if dancing together.

The friends dipped their heads, slowed their fluttering wings and glided lower. They could see hundreds of animals, birds and other woodland creatures filling the glade, their chatter like a woodland orchestra.

"It looks as if the whole wood is here!" Katie said, her eyes alight. She couldn't wait to meet everyone.

Alex came to a hovering stop in the sky, her beak trembling.

Eva flew to her friend and reached out a wing. "Don't be shy, Alex. Let's go and meet them. They're really happy for us to be here, remember?"

Alex gave Eva a small smile. She was

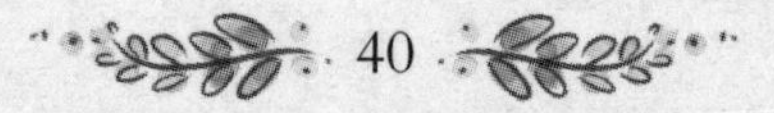

right, of course. The three friends flew down in gentle circles. Katie and Alex landed delicately on the soft grassy ground. Eva wasn't quite so graceful, somehow skidding to a stop just in front of Bobby.

"Ah, excellent – you found it." He put out a paw to help Eva up. "Please, allow me to introduce you to everyone." The badger ushered them over to one side of the grass circle, where the ground sloped upwards, backed by a line of gorgeous baby-pink foxgloves.

"It's just like a stage!" Katie flung out her wings and twirled towards it.

As she hopped along behind Katie, Alex heard the crowd oohing and aahing.

"Look, they're beautiful!" a deer whispered.

Alex quickly realized why – the

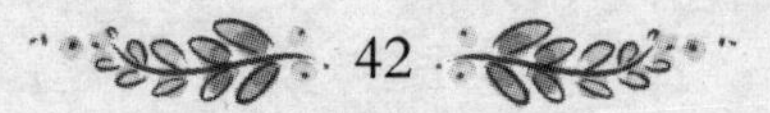

Blossom Wood animals were excited about their arrival! She wondered if her feathery cheeks had gone red. She wasn't used to being in the limelight.

"I can't believe it – the owls are really here," said a little grey bunny at the front of the audience.

"It's a miracle!" squeaked a ladybird as she zoomed into the glade.

Katie, Eva and Alex stood in a line on the sloped stage while Bobby addressed the crowd. "Ahem. I said, AHEM!" The excited chatter dimmed to whispers. "That's better. Now, dearest animals and birds of Blossom Wood—"

"Hey, what about us insects?" interrupted a wriggling caterpillar at the front.

"Sorry, Wilf." The badger raised his bushy eyebrows at the little green creature.

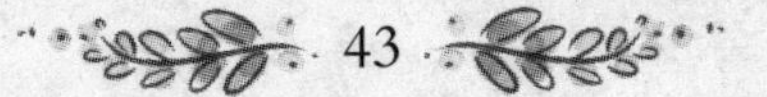

"Animals, birds *and insects* of Blossom Wood, we've been waiting a terribly long time for this. I am honoured, delighted and thrilled to introduce to you Katie, Eva and Alex, the newly arrived owls of Blossom Wood!"

The glade erupted in a booming round of applause. The rabbits bounced up and down like space hoppers, the squirrels jumped around and waved their tails crazily, the butterflies fluttered and spun and the bees swarmed in circles. The frogs clapped their bellies, the deer clapped their hooves and the woodpeckers clapped their wings. The wrens and robins flew over to the owls and touched their beaks to theirs in a sign of welcome. Katie stretched out her wings and sank into a curtsy, not knowing quite what else to do!

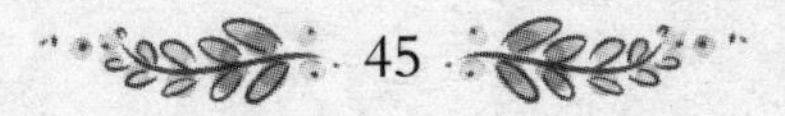

Bobby hadn't finished yet. "Listen, please! The owls are here just in time, for our beloved Moon Chestnut is very, very ill. Its branches have stopped growing and the leaves are brown and lifeless – and it's getting worse every day. I'm sure it's going to die soon if we don't do something!"

The crowd began murmuring amongst themselves:

"Not our wonderful tree!"

"What will happen to our nest?"

"Where we will live if it dies?"

"What will we do without it?"

"Wait!" Bobby held up a paw and the concerned voices of the woodland creatures grew silent. "There's no need to worry. The wise owls are here to help us, so we can be sure it will be saved!"

Alex shifted from one leg to the other, her head full of worries. She certainly wanted to help, but she had no idea how they would be able to. *And everyone's relying on us!* she thought.

More applause echoed around Foxglove Glade. A bee buzzed over to the stage and whispered into Bobby's ear.

"This is Bella," Bobby relayed to Alex,

Eva and Katie. "She's incredibly shy, but she asked me to tell you that if you can help save the chestnut tree, home to her family's beehive for generations, she promises you unlimited honey, for ever."

Katie didn't know what else to say but, "Thank you, Bella. We'll try our very best!"

Chapter 4
Good News and Bad News

Katie, Eva and Alex stood in front of the Moon Chestnut tree, looking it up and down. They'd flown straight back there after the meeting, still with no ideas about how they could save the tree. Underneath was a patchwork of brown leaves that had fallen from it. The thin branches drooped almost to the ground

and the tree creaked as it moved in the gentle breeze, as if it really were taking its last breaths.

Alex was staring at the peeling bark on the trunk, which looked like old, frail wallpaper, when she heard a different sound. It wasn't the creaking tree, but a whistling from beneath her. She gazed around, but she couldn't see any animals or insects about. What *was* it? "Can you hear that whistling?" she asked her friends. Eva and Katie tilted their heads left and right, then nodded.

"Where's it coming from?" said Eva.

Katie followed the sound, fluttering towards a blackberry hedge, with Eva and Alex at her tail. The whistling still floated up from the ground, and now they detected a sort of scraping noise too.

Eva brushed some of the chestnut

leaves away from the ground with her wing. She froze, mid-sweep. She'd uncovered a hole in the ground! In it stood a black mole, glaring at them, his hands on his hips.

"Oi! Who's there, disturbing my tunnel-digging like that? Go AWAY! Leave me alone!" His little spectacles wobbled on his little pink nose as he squeaked.

Shocked, the friends hopped away quickly and huddled behind the blackberry bush to talk. "Do you think the mole has his tunnels all round the tree?" whispered Eva, her green eyes as big as chestnuts.

Alex remembered something she'd read in one of her wildlife books. "If he has, then the tunnels would have disturbed the tree roots. That's why it's dying! We have to ask him to stop."

Katie nodded, feeling determined, and fluttered back to the mole. "Erm … hello. I'm Katie." She flapped a wing in greeting. "We're sorry to bother you, but we think your tunnels are making the chestnut tree ill. We're afraid it will die soon, and we know how important it is to Blossom Wood. Do you think you could stop tunnelling here, and move

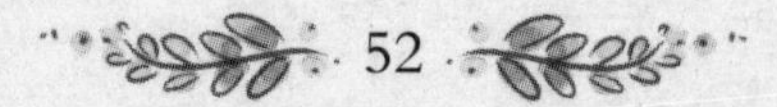

somewhere else, please?"

"MOVE SOMEWHERE ELSE?" The mole raised his voice to a whole new level of squeak and his whiskers shook. "No way! I'm fed up with getting told off and being asked to move all the time. What's wrong with tunnels, anyway? Digging is great!" As if to demonstrate, he began pawing at the soil with his large spade-like hands, sending grit everywhere.

"It's not that we don't like tunnels," twittered Alex softly, ducking the flying soil. "It's just—"

"I'M NOT MOVING!" the mole squeak-shouted again. "And who are you, anyway?" He whipped off his glasses and squinted. "I've never seen you around here. Go back to where you came from!"

Eva opened her little pink beak to

say something, but the mole had already scampered backwards, tail first, deep into his network of tunnels.

Alex poked her head into the hole, but all she could see was pitch-black soil and a few worms wiggling about. "He's gone," Alex told her friends. "Now what do we do?"

"How are you getting on?" came a gravelly voice.

They turned round to see Bobby padding towards them.

"The good news is that we've found out the problem," Katie told the old badger. "There's a mole burrowing tunnels all round the Moon Chestnut's roots!"

"The bad news is that when we asked him to move, he refused," added Eva.

Bobby put a paw to his forehead. "Oh treetops! I can guess precisely which mole it is – Pete! I'm afraid he's been quite a nuisance to his neighbours in Blossom Wood. He tunnels here, there and everywhere, with no thought for his fellow woodlanders. The trouble is, he's terribly hard to talk to – he likes to be by himself, you see, hidden away."

Alex suddenly thought of something. It was unfair of them to ask Pete to move when he didn't have a new home to go to. "Wait – we can't just chuck him out and make him homeless! We have to find him somewhere new to live first. Maybe if we did that, we could persuade him to leave the chestnut tree alone."

Katie raised her large wings in a shrug. "But where?"

"That's a very good question." Bobby scratched his white-tipped ear. "Not many animals will want a mole tunnelling near them."

They fell silent, trying to come up with ideas. Eva thought back to their journey to Foxglove Glade, remembering the fields and forests they'd passed. She was soon absorbed in her daydream, reliving their flight high over the treetops, watching the scenery whizz past below. She jumped when she realized someone was nudging her.

"Are you OK, Eva?" Alex asked, her yellow eyes wide with concern.

"Oh yes, I was just thinking… There's a big patch of empty ground to the right of Willow Lake, isn't there, Bobby?"

The badger nodded. "We call it the Brown Desert. I don't think anyone lives there – there are no trees, no bushes, not even grass…"

"Then it would be perfect for Pete!"

Alex did a little jump, and her feathers rustled. "What a brilliant idea, Eva."

Bobby stroked his chin. "Yes, you're right! Oh, I knew you wise, wonderful owls would be able to help us! Thank you so, SO much." The badger bounced over and, to the friends' surprise, wrapped his arms around them in a group hug.

"Right," hooted Katie as they broke away, "we've got work to do. Let's put Plan Move Pete into action!"

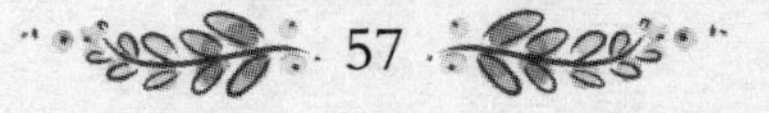

Chapter 5

Plan Move Pete

The owls decided it would be best to split up. Eva flew to the Brown Desert, as Bobby had called it, to check it would be all right for Pete to move there. They didn't want to disturb the home of anyone else – that would just make things worse.

When she arrived, she spotted a herd

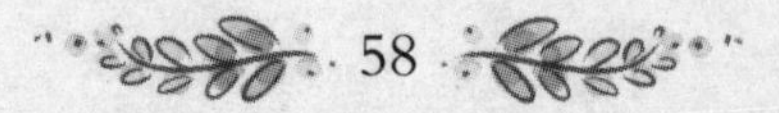

of deer roaming around the edges. Eva explained the situation.

The mother deer nodded her silky brown head. "No one actually lives here – we just come to the Brown Desert to stretch our legs," she told Eva in a smooth voice. "We won't mind a few tunnels, and we're very careful – we'll make sure our hooves don't squash them."

Meanwhile, Alex was searching for a colony of rabbits that Bobby had told her lived beside Willow Lake. She found their deep burrow holes on the shore of the lake between the shimmering willow trees. She bobbed her head up and down nervously, worried about asking for their help, but Bobby had promised they were friendly.

"Hello – is anyone there?" she asked politely, not wanting to anger the rabbits the way they had Pete.

A fluffy grey rabbit about the same size as Alex popped her head out of one of the dark holes. Then another head appeared from a different hole, followed by a third, and a fourth. Before she knew it, ten pairs of cute rabbit eyes were looking at her. They all grinned, showing their long white teeth.

"It's Alex, isn't it!" said the first bunny, who had large, pointy ears. "Oh, what an honour to have an owl visit our home! I'd have tidied if I'd known! I'm Ruby. And these are my kids … well, a few of them, anyway – there are a lot more inside!"

Ruby was so welcoming, Alex stopped feeling shy. She told Ruby about the problem. "So we were wondering … please could you dig some tunnels to help prepare Pete's new home?"

Ruby's nose twitched and her black eyes gleamed. "We'd love to help, wouldn't we, kids! I'm sure we can create something special for him." The mother bunny beckoned to her brood of children, and the rabbits began darting out of their burrow holes towards the barren Brown Desert.

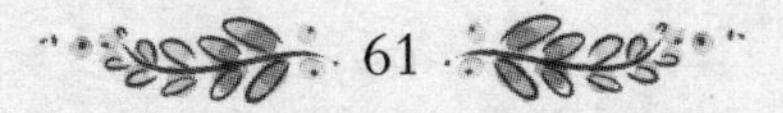

One particularly tiny bunny hung back. He hopped up to Alex shyly. "My name's Billy," he said, in a voice even smaller than Alex's. "I can't believe you're really here. I have always wanted to meet an owl!"

Alex smiled and put out her wing to shake his paw. "It's lovely to meet you, Billy. My name's Alex." She couldn't help thinking that the rabbit looked a lot like Eva's drawing.

Billy tilted his furry head up, his brown eyes full of awe. "Can we be friends?" he squeaked. "Will you come back to play with me another day?"

"Of course I will." Alex grinned at the sweet bunny. "But for now, will you help build Pete's new home?"

Billy nodded solemnly. "Yes – I'll do anything to help you!" With that, he waved a paw and scampered off to join his brothers and sisters.

With her part of the plan in action, Alex fluttered her wings and soared up into the sky. She looked down at the rabbits already busy digging at the ground. She felt glad they had so much energy. Pete's new home would be built in no time!

Back at the chestnut tree, Katie worked on the final part of their plan. She was gathering blackberries – Pete's

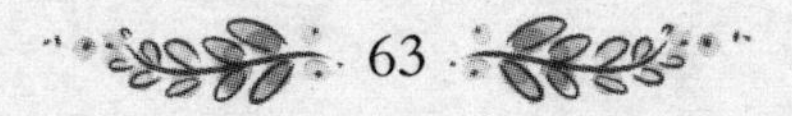

favourite snack, according to Bobby – and asking any passing butterflies and birds if they could help. Luckily they were all willing to give Katie a hand, and the creatures flew back and forth from the blackberry bushes, bringing Katie the fruit, while she laid out a path beginning at the entrance to Pete's tunnels. It wasn't long before she'd made a winding line of little juicy

blackberries that stretched across Blossom Wood. Starting at the chestnut tree, it wound through the forest and across a log bridge over a river, ending up at the Brown Desert beside Willow Lake.

With each of their parts of the plan complete, the three friends gathered together at the foot of the Moon Chestnut. There was one last problem: they knew that Pete would *never* come out of his hole if he was surrounded by the creatures of Blossom Wood.

"We've got to hide!" Alex tweeted. She, Katie and Eva passed the message on from bird to insect to animal, until everyone had hidden behind trees, in branches, beneath hedges or among long grasses. Blossom Wood became so quiet, it seemed as if even the leaves on the trees had stopped rustling.

With her wingtip Katie pushed a final blackberry into the entrance of Pete's tunnels. Then she zoomed up to the branches of a sycamore tree to hide with Alex and Eva.

Everyone held their breath, and waited.

And waited.

Alex didn't even blink, she was concentrating so hard on Pete's tunnel. This was their best chance of saving the Moon Chestnut. What if it didn't work?

"Where is he?" whispered Katie, turning to her friends. "Maybe the blackberries aren't enough to get him out of there! Perhaps we should have tried something else..."

"Wait a minute," mouthed Eva. "Look!"

Katie looked back at the tunnel entrance. Her incredible owl eyesight meant she could see the ground perfectly,

even from this high up. A tiny pink nose was twitching at the edge of the hole … followed by silvery whiskers! Then came Pete's little round glasses and squinty eyes. But what would he do next?

Chapter 6

There's Mole Place Like Home

Alex's head bobbed up and down. *Please, Pete, follow the path!* She almost couldn't bear to look. When the mole darted out of the tunnel and gobbled up the first blackberry in one bite, Alex squeezed her beak shut so she wouldn't let out a squeal of relief.

Pete crinkled his nose to sniff the air,

then ran forward to the next blackberry. He put out his paws to feel the little round fruit and smiled. "Oh yum!" he squealed, plucking it up and dropping it into his mouth.

Eva let out a long breath, realizing she'd been holding it as they waited. Pete kept going – from the third blackberry to the fourth, to the fifth... Soon he must have eaten more than a hundred blackberries, Eva guessed – and he showed no signs of stopping.

The owls could see the whole path of blackberries from their position in the sycamore tree, and they watched with thudding hearts as Pete drew closer and closer to his new home. They still didn't dare speak. In fact, Blossom Wood was totally silent except for the regular *munch, gulp, munch, gulp* coming from Pete.

After gulping down the fruits scattered over the log bridge, he finally reached the edge of the Brown Desert. There, an old tree branch lay on its side. It was engraved with the words:

Pete's Pad
No. 1 The Brown Desert
There's mole place like home!

The letters were surrounded by pretty carvings of flowers and leaves.

"Did you make the sign?" Alex whispered to Eva. "It's beautiful."

Eva's heart-shaped face widened in a beam. "Yes. Thank you!"

The little mole stopped close to the sign, and squinted through his glasses to read it. He grinned, wiggled his whiskers and clapped his paws together in delight.

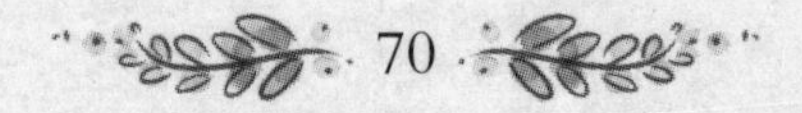

Then he scampered into the tunnel, his shovel-hands pawing at the soil as he went.

"This is fun!" Katie heard Pete squeak-shout and wondered what he meant. She stared harder at Pete's new home and chuckled. It looked as if the rabbits hadn't just dug a few tunnels for Pete – they'd made him an incredible mole adventure playground, with roller-coaster tunnels, slides and swings.

"We did it!" hooted Katie, high-fiving Alex and Eva with each wing before flying up into the sky. "You can come out now," she called to the Blossom Wood creatures. "Well done, everyone – we couldn't have done this without you!"

Eva fluttered up to join her. "Now, will you help us fill the tunnels around the Moon Chestnut?"

A big cheer went up. "YES!" the woodlanders replied. All the animals, birds and insects of Blossom Wood emerged from their hiding places and ran, flew, buzzed or trotted to the sad-looking chestnut tree.

"OK, everyone," said Katie, taking charge. "Let's do this!"

They all leapt into action. Soil was

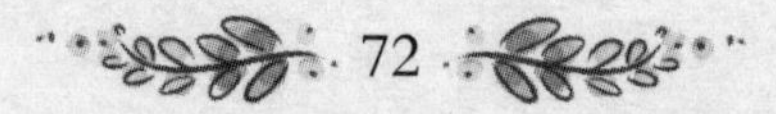

soon flying everywhere. The animals tipped, threw, pushed, pulled, flung and shovelled the soil back into the holes. Foxes sprinted, rabbits scampered, deer dashed and squirrels darted.

Without any paws, the owls couldn't do much to help move the soil into the holes, but they could use their brilliant eyesight to spot any tunnels that still needed filling. They flew around the tree, giving advice and shouting encouragement to the woodland residents who were working so very hard.

"That's it, Wilf!"

"Brilliant work, Billy!"

"Bobby – there's a hole, just to your left!"

The sun had just dipped below the horizon when the last hole was filled. The sky had turned purple, the moon rose

above the trees and the first stars were beginning to twinkle like fairy lights.

Katie, Eva and Alex landed alongside the worn-out animals. "That was fantastic!" Alex flapped her little wings in happiness.

"Thank you so much!" tweeted Eva.

When the friends held wingtips and looked up at the tree, the sight was magical. The branches seemed thicker and stronger already. The bark no longer flaked, instead shining in the moonlight. The leaves were much less brown – and Alex could see some new, bright-green shoots sprouting near the top of the tall, curving tree.

A buzzing-humming sound filled the air, until a cloud of bees and birds appeared in front of the owls. "My name's Winnie," said a pretty brown

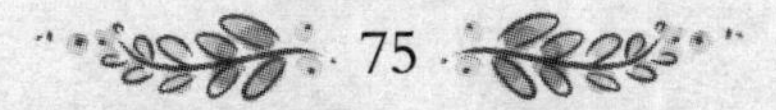

wren. "From the very, very bottom of our wing-diddle-lings and on behalf of every single bird of this great, grand chestnut tree, thank you, thank you, *thank you.*"

Bella zoomed towards them next, and flew right up to Alex's ear. "The bees all say a big buzzing thank you too," she whispered. "You must come and taste our honey soon. Remember, you can have all the honey you want!"

"Thank you!" A warm, happy feeling spread through Alex. She felt honoured that the bee had spoken to her despite being so shy.

Loulou appeared, her tail swishing back and forth. "And thank you from all the squirrels," she squeaked. "We're sure lots of tasty chestnuts will soon be back on the tree! Oh look, there's one already.

You must have it!" She shot towards the Moon Chestnut and ran up the trunk, plucking the chestnut from a low-hanging branch. Scampering back down, Loulou tore off the prickly shell and pushed the shiny brown nut into one of Eva's talons.

Eva held it tight. "Thank you, Loulou."

"Do you think we should go home now?" Alex asked her two best friends. "I'm worried Mum will be back from work and wondering where I am…"

"Do we have to? It's so magical here!" Katie spun on the spot, her snowy wings flying out wide. She wasn't sure she ever wanted to leave.

Eva thought for a moment before replying, "I'd love to stay, but Alex is probably right. We should get home before it gets too dark." She turned to the creatures of Blossom Wood. "It's been amazing to meet you all."

"We can come and visit again soon, can't we?" Alex asked Bobby.

Bobby nodded his black-and-white head furiously. "Oh yes. I don't know what we'd do without you now! From the tips of my toes to the treetops, thank you for everything."

"We'll be back whenever you

need us," Eva promised.

"But how will we know when to come?" asked Katie.

"That's easy – I'll send the feather to you as a sign," Bobby's deep voice croaked.

Thank treetops they'd be able to come back! Eva, Alex and Katie couldn't imagine life without Blossom Wood. They'd had the most incredible adventure, and met some wonderful new friends.

"Goodbye, everybody!" Katie waved one of her huge white wings before flapping off slowly into the darkening sky. Alex and Eva quickly followed, fluttering their wings to the animals and creatures below. The woodlanders all waved back. From above, they looked like a sea of swishing paws, wings and tails.

"I hope this works!" said Alex as they

stood on the high Moon Chestnut branch holding wingtips. They squeezed their eyes tight and their ears filled with a great whooshing sound. Just like before, they spun round and round and round. Alex felt as if she were inside a tumble dryer – although at least she wasn't so scared this time.

Their feathers tingled, their beaks itched and their talons tickled, until the spinning died down.

Katie opened her eyes. "We're back!"

Eva and Alex blinked their eyes open too. Sure enough, they were sitting inside the large hollow tree trunk, girls once more, with not a wing or a feather in sight. Though it felt a bit strange to have skin and clothes again, after so long as feathery owls!

"Katie, Eva, Alex, where are you?" came

Alfie's voice. "My cartoon's finished and I want to play!"

Alex smiled. "We've come back at the exact moment we left!" She paused. "It's almost as if our trip to Blossom Wood never happened..." The smile slipped from her face as she worried that perhaps it never had. Could it have been just an amazing dream?

Eva patted her jeans pocket and

winked. "Except for this," she said, pulling out the little shiny chestnut Loulou had given her. "We really did go to Blossom Wood. And I can't wait to go back!"

Did You Know?

- Just as Pete does in the story, moles actually can run backwards! They have very bad eyesight, so they use their excellent sense of touch and their sensitive whiskers to get around.
- Little owls really do bob their head a lot, just as Alex does when she becomes a little owl. And, like Alex, they're usually shy, too!
- Rabbits' teeth never stop growing – which is why they're so long.
- You might remember from the story that a group of deer is called a herd. Other groups of animals known as herds are elephants, giraffes, goats and cows. A group of foxes is called a skulk, a group of moles is known as a labour and a group of frogs is an army!

Look out for more

The Owls of Blossom Wood

adventures!

The Owls of Blossom Wood

To the Rescue

Catherine Coe

The Owls of Blossom Wood

Lost and Found

Catherine Coe

Would you like more animal fun and facts?

Fancy flying across the treetops in the Owls of Blossom Wood game?

Want sneak peeks of other books in the series?

Then check out the Owls of Blossom Wood website at:

theowlsofblossomwood.com